KV-575-619

The worst thing about my mum is . . .

She's always rushing,

calling,

shaking,

pulling,

pushing.

She drags me out of bed at eight. It's . . .

"Put your arms up. Stick your foot out.
Come on, Sam, we'll all be late."

I'm still asleep

At breakfast Mum says, "Don't be slow.

Sam, eat your toast. Sam, drink your milk.

Still eating

Sam, please be quick, it's time to go."

We race . . . . to get . . . .

She heaves . . . . and . . . . tugs . . . .

We're late . . . . The clock . . . .

. . . . .to school . . . . .on time. . . . .

. . . . .I pant . . . . .and . . . . .puff.

Gotta pain

. . . . .begins . . . . .to chime. . . . .

I hate it, shopping with my mum.

Don't like shopping

She zips in here, then zooms in there.
I drag behind and suck my thumb.

We're home at last, she still won't stop. It's...

"Eat your beans up. Drink your orange. Sam, you haven't had a drop."

But at two o'clock the doorbell rings. It's Jane!

Mum . . .

can we paint?

Or paddle?

Will you push us on the swings?

I'm drinking my tea

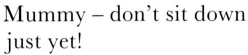

Mummy – don't sit down just yet!

Where's my Lego?
Where's my wellies?

Sam, I'm tired

Can you find my fishing net?

Come on, Mum, we want a drink,
some crisps . . . a Smartie . . . a picnic . . . a party.
Can we play boats in the sink?

The worst thing about that Sam is . . .

He's always rushing,

He never stops!

calling,   shaking,   pulling, pushing.

There's just one thing wrong with our dad . . .

He doesn't like teasing,

fighting   and fooling,

If he's
in a mood

snuggling   and squeezing.

When he wakes up . . .

we climb in bed. "Don't jump," he moans. "Don't bounce," he groans.

"Will you two girls get off my head!"

It's like
a circus

It's like a pigsty!

At breakfast time we mess about.
We stir, we swish, we flood the dish!
Our dad looks up. He starts to shout.

Dad works all day – it isn't fair.

We wave and call, we shout and bawl.

It's like a football match

He tells us off, "You rowdy pair."

We're dressing up; Dad's on the phone.
I start to wiggle and then we giggle.
"Clear off," he says. "Leave me alone."

It's like a pantomime

We're playing cars while Dad makes tea.

It's like a racetrack

We rrrev,   we hmmm,   we brum, brum, brrrmmm.

Dad nearly trips – he glares at me.

But later, when *he* wants to play
and we're twisting, twirling, wheeling, whirling . . .

We're not sure we like it

You watch – he'll soon get carried away.

He picks us up and carries us off,
squawking and squealing up to the ceiling.
"3–2–1 . . . We have Blast Off!"

Then he tucks us in.
"That's one. That's two."

He crawls, he creeps, he taps, he peeps.

He tiptoes in and goes "Whoooooooo!"

There's just one thing wrong with those girls . . .

They don't like teasing,

When they' in a mood

fighting and fooling, snuggling and squeezing.